SHARKS: HUNTERS of the DEEP™

THE WHALE SHARK
GENTLE GIANT

JOANNE RANDOLPH

PowerKIDS
press.

New York

Published in 2007 by The Rosen Publishing Group, Inc.
29 East 21st Street, New York, NY 10010

First Edition

Book Design: Greg Tucker and Dean Galiano
Photo Researcher: Sam Cha

Photo Credits: Cover, p. 1 © Brian J. Skerry/Getty Images; pp. 4, 6 © James D. Watt/SeaPics.com; p. 8 © GeoAtlas; p. 10 © Ron & Valerie Taylor/SeaPics.com; p. 12 © Digital Stock; p. 14 © Bob Cranston/SeaPics.com; p. 16 © Toshifumi Kiamura/AFP/Getty Images; p. 18 © Marc Bernardi/SeaPics.com; p. 20 © www.istockphoto.com/Harold Bolton.

Library of Congress Cataloging-in-Publication Data

Randolph, Joanne.
    The whale shark : gentle giant / Joanne Randolph. — 1st ed.
      p. cm. — (Sharks—hunters of the deep)
    Includes bibliographical references and index.
    ISBN-13: 978-1-4042-3626-4 (library binding : alk. paper)
    ISBN-10: 1-4042-3626-0 (library binding : alk. paper)
    1. Whale shark—Juvenile literature. I. Title.
    QL638.95.R4R36 2007
    597.3—dc22
                                                          2006019526

Manufactured in the United States of America

CONTENTS

MEET THE WHALE SHARK

What is as big as a whale, but not a whale at all? The answer is a whale shark. Whales are **mammals** and cannot breathe underwater. The whale shark looks a lot like a whale, but it is a fish, not a mammal. In fact it is the largest fish in the ocean. It can be 40 feet (12 m) long or more, and it weighs up to 20 tons (18 t). That is a really big fish!

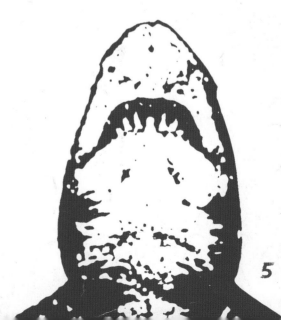

THE WHALE SHARK BREATHES USING GILLS, JUST LIKE OTHER FISH. GILLS ARE SPECIAL BODY PARTS THAT LET AN ANIMAL BREATHE UNDERWATER.

Mystery Markings

Whale sharks have special markings on their grayish, bluish, or brownish skin. Their skin has light lines on it that form many squares. Inside each square is a light dot. The markings look like sunlight on the ocean waves. Though large whale sharks do not need to hide from other animals, their smaller babies do. Their markings might keep the babies safe from animals that want to eat them. No one knows for sure.

Whale sharks have tiny, toothlike points all over their skin, just as other sharks do. They also have the thickest skin in the world.

7

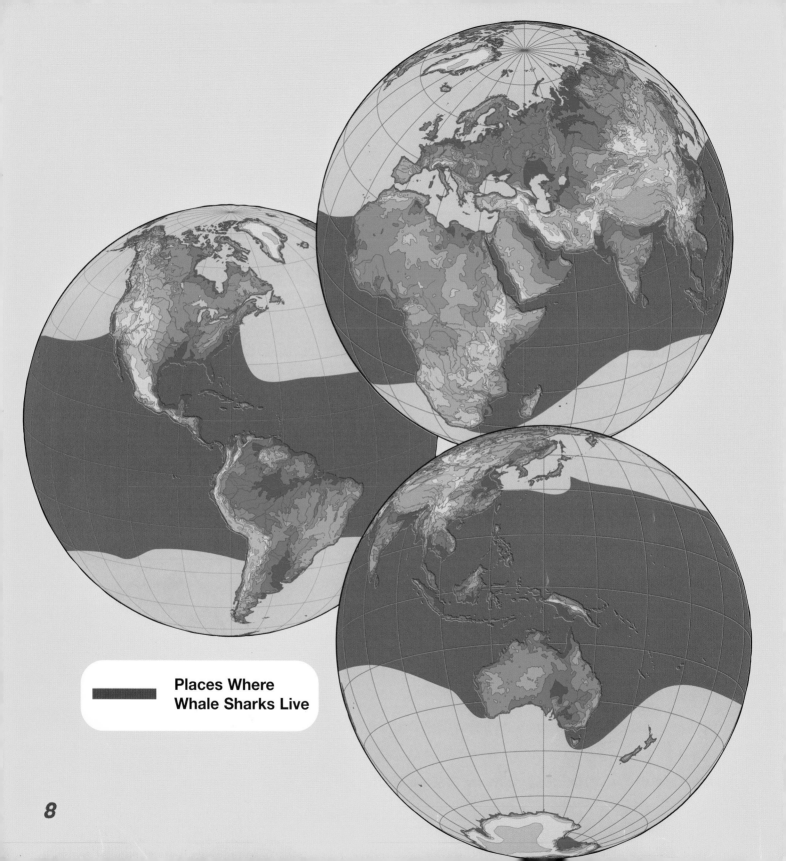

**Places Where
Whale Sharks Live**

WHALE SHARK HOMES

Whale sharks can be found in most oceans around the world. They like warm waters best. They can be found as far north as New York and Japan. They swim as far south as Brazil, Chile, Australia, and Hawaii. They can be seen swimming close to shore and far out in the ocean.

Whale sharks do not make one place their home. People think whale sharks **migrate** a long way to find food or to have their babies.

THIS MAP SHOWS THE PLACES WHERE THE WHALE SHARK SWIMS. IT MOVES TO FIND WARMER WATERS AND TO FIND PLACES WITH A LOT OF FOOD.

TEETH THAT DO NOT BITE?

Whale sharks are sharks. Sharks have lots of teeth they use to catch and eat **prey**, right? Whale sharks do have a lot of teeth. In fact they can have 4,000 teeth in their mouth at one time. This is more than other sharks have. Whale sharks' teeth are too small to catch or bite prey, though. Each tiny tooth is only about as big as half a grain of rice.

WHALE SHARKS HAVE **300** ROWS OF TEETH. NO ONE IS SURE WHY THESE SHARKS HAVE SO MANY TEETH.

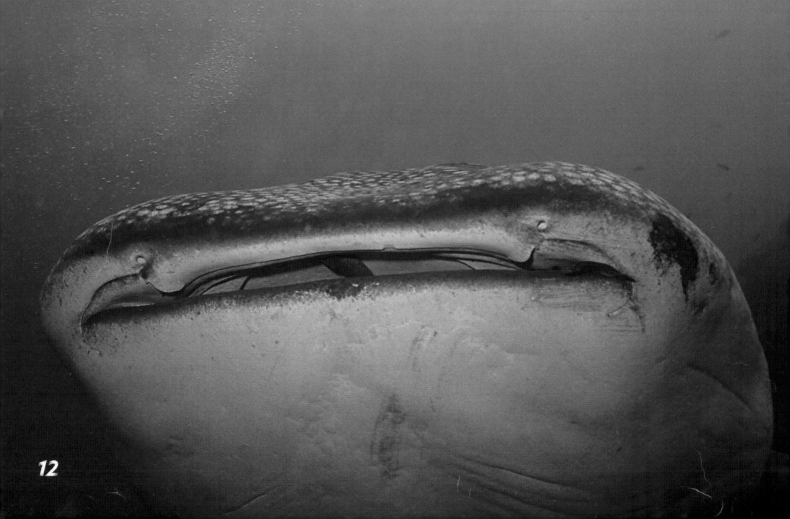

What's for Dinner?

You might think that such a huge fish would need to eat lots of large animals to stay alive. The whale shark eats the smallest animals in the ocean, though. These animals are called **plankton**. Plankton are so small that a person cannot see them without using a special tool. The whale shark also eats small fish, crabs, and other tiny animals. It does much of its feeding at the end of the day or at night.

THE MOUTH OF A WHALE SHARK IS 6 FEET (2 M) WIDE. THIS IS BIG ENOUGH FOR MOST PEOPLE TO FIT INSIDE!

HUNTING BY SMELL

Whale sharks do not use their eyes to spot prey. In fact they have very small eyes and cannot see very well. Instead whale sharks use their **sense** of smell to help them find their tiny prey.

Once the shark knows where the food is, it opens its huge mouth wide. It sucks water into its mouth. This carries the prey with it. The prey is caught on the special combs on the whale shark's **gills**.

WATER PASSES THROUGH AND LEAVES THE SHARK'S BODY THROUGH THE GILL SLITS. GILL SLITS ARE OPENINGS ON THE SIDES OF A FISH'S BODY.

ENEMIES OF THE WHALE SHARK

The whale shark is so big that it does not have much to fear from other ocean animals. Whale shark babies have to be careful, though. Young whale sharks have been found in the stomachs of blue sharks and blue marlins. Once the whale shark grows to its full size, people are its only real enemy. It is hunted for its **liver**, which is used for oil. It is also hunted for its meat and its fins.

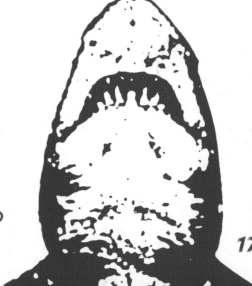

IN JAPAN THIS SHARK IS KEPT IN AQUARIUMS, WHERE PEOPLE CAN SEE THE HUGE FISH AND LEARN MORE ABOUT IT. IT IS HARD TO KEEP THIS SHARK IN AN AQUARIUM BECAUSE OF ITS LARGE SIZE AND THE KIND OF FOOD IT EATS.

BIRTH OF A GIANT

Whale sharks are huge fish, but they start out life quite small. Whale shark babies are about 21 inches (53 cm) long. A whale shark mother carries hundreds of baby sharks inside eggs in her body. Only some of the eggs will become baby sharks, though. The mother carries the eggs until the babies are ready to be born. Then she gives birth to up to 300 live pups.

WHALE SHARKS LIVE ON THEIR OWN FROM THE TIME THEY ARE BORN. WHALE SHARKS MAY LIVE AS LONG AS 60 OR EVEN 100 YEARS.

GENTLE GIANT

Many people think sharks are scary and mean. Whale sharks are **gentle** giants, though. Even if they wanted to eat a person, their throats are not big enough. Generally these sharks just mind their own business. Many people pay to swim with these sharks in the waters off Australia or other places. It is important to treat these fish with **respect**, though. They need to be left alone to hunt and live their lives.

HERE DIVERS SWIM WITH A WHALE SHARK IN THE WATERS OFF MALDIVES. MALDIVES IS A STRING OF ISLANDS IN SOUTHERN ASIA.

KEEPING THE WHALE SHARK SAFE

Whale sharks could be in danger if too many people fish for these sharks. Many places have made it against the law to hunt for these fish. We do not know how many whale sharks there are. We do know that we should keep this beautiful giant safe. By learning about the whale shark, you are taking the first step toward helping it live in the world's oceans for a long time to come.

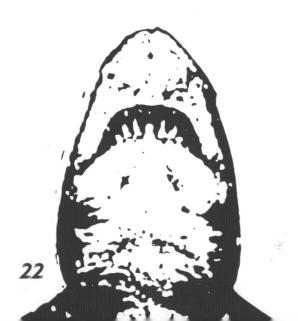

GLOSSARY

gentle (JEN-tul) Peaceful.

gills (GILZ) Body parts that fish use for breathing.

liver (LIH-ver) The part of the body that makes and stores sugar. People use the oil in fish livers.

mammals (MA-mulz) Warm-blooded animals that have a backbone and hair, breathe air, and feed milk to their young.

migrate (MY-grayt) To move from one place to another.

plankton (PLANK-ten) Plants and animals that drift with the movement of the water.

prey (PRAY) An animal that is hunted by another animal for food.

respect (rih-SPEKT) To think highly of someone or something.

sense (SENS) One of the five ways we learn about the world. The senses are taste, smell, touch, hearing, and sight.

INDEX

B
babies, 7, 9, 17, 19

E
eggs, 19
eyes, 15

F
fins, 17
fish, 5, 13, 19, 21–22
food, 9, 15

G
gills, 15

L
liver, 17

M
mammal(s), 5
markings, 7

O
ocean(s), 5, 7, 9, 13, 17, 22

P
people, 9, 21–22
plankton, 13

prey, 11, 15
pups, 19

S
sense, 15
skin, 7

T
teeth, 11

W
whale(s), 5

WEB SITES

Due to the changing nature of Internet links, PowerKids Press has developed an online list of Web sites related to the subject of this book. This site is updated regularly. Please use this link to access the list: www.powerkidslinks.com/sharks/whale/